For James, Diego, Emma, Peregryn, Juniper,
Dyson, Kate, Jayden, Hailey, Zoey and every
new hue mixed into the spectrum

First published 2018 by Henry Holt
This edition first published in the UK 2018 by Macmillan Children's Books
an imprint of Pan Macmillan,
20 New Wharf Road, London N1 9RR
Associated companies throughout the world
www.panmacmillan.com

ISBN 978-1-5098-7133-9 (HB)
ISBN 978-1-5098-7134-6 (PB)

Text and illustrations copyright © Arree Chung 2018

The right of Arree Chung to be identified as the author and illustrator of this work has been asserted by him
in accordance with the Copyright, Designs and Patents Act 1988.

1 3 5 7 9 8 6 4 2

A CIP catalogue record for this book is available
from the British Library.

Printed in China.

MIXED

Arree Chung

An inspiring story about colour

Macmillan Children's Books

In the beginning, there were three colours:

Yellows,

Reds

and Blues.

Reds were the loudest...

... Yellows were the brightest...

... and Blues were the coolest.

Everyone lived in colour harmony, until...

... one afternoon,
when a Red said,

The Blues were too cool
to even respond.

But then, one day, a Yellow noticed a Blue.

And something happened.

Yellow and Blue became inseparable.

Life felt so vibrant!

But not all the colours were happy about it.

But Yellow and Blue loved each
other so much, they decided to

Together, they created a new colour.

They named her Green.

Green was bright like Yellow

and calm like Blue,

but really she was
a colour all of her own.

Everyone was fascinated.

Even the grumpy colours fell in love with Green.

The colours began to see new possibilities.

Soon, other colours mixed

and mixed...

... and mixed

and mixed!

There were so many new colours. And a lot of new names.

The old neighbourhoods of Redville, Blue Town and Yellow Heights didn't make sense anymore. Everyone wanted to live together, so they rebuilt the city.

The new city was full of colour.

It wasn't perfect,

but it was home.